ReadZone Books Limited

www.ReadZoneBooks.com

© in this edition 2016 ReadZone Books Limited

This print edition published in cooperation with Fiction Express, who first
published this title in weekly instalments as an interactive e-book.

Fiction Express
Boolino Limited
First Floor Office, 2 College Street,
Ludlow, Shropshire SY8 1AN
www.fictionexpress.co.uk

Find out more about Fiction Express on pages 96–97.

Design: Laura Harrison & Keith Williams
Cover Image: Bigstock

© in the text 2016 Tommy Donbavand
The moral right of the author has been asserted.

ISBN 978-1-78322-602-3

Printed in Malta by Melita Press

BLAST
TO THE PAST
A Stone Age Adventure

TOMMY DONBAVAND

FICTION
EXPRESS

What do other readers think?

Here are some comments left on the Fiction Express blog about this book:

"I really like this book because there's lots of interesting words; also it's full of action :-)"
Nathaniel, Ludlow Junior School

"I just love this book and will read and read it again and again… WOW!"
Nikola, Kingston, London

"We are enjoying Blast to the Past*! We like the way they were transported to the past. We are looking forward to reading the final chapter!"*
Birch Class, Gobowen Primary School

"I love this book and I want to read more!!!"
Keyleigh, Telford

Contents

To the real Sam and Alissa – many adventures!

Chapter 1

Cave

"Come out now, Alissa!" cried Sam, his voice echoing off the stone walls of the cave. "You know we're not supposed to go any deeper!"

There was no reply.

"Alissa! Come back!"

Nothing.

With a sigh, Sam switched on his torch and ducked under the low rock that marked the part of the ancient cave system he and his friends had been told they should never go beyond. All around him, he could hear the steady drip dripping of water falling from the roof of the cave onto the slippery, slimy rocks below. He shivered. It was cold down here, even under his thick winter coat.

"Where are you, Ali?"

Suddenly, a second torch switched on and a face appeared right in front of him. "Boo!"

Sam jumped. "What did you do that for?"

Alissa shrugged in the semi-darkness. "It's funny."

"Not to me it isn't!" Sam hissed. "And neither is going further into the caves than we're allowed – it's dangerous."

"Oh, come on…" said Alissa, swinging her torch beam down into the darkness ahead. "Where's your sense of adventure? There could be anything down there – hidden treasure, or a smuggler's den. Anything! We should explore."

"No, we *shouldn't*!" insisted Sam.

Alissa scowled. "You're not my boss!"

"Maybe not," Sam admitted, "but I am older by six weeks, so I'm in charge."

"Says who?"

"Says me!" said Sam firmly. "I mean it, Ali – if you take one more step…."

Alissa grinned. "What? You mean like this…."

Turning to face the blackness, Alissa took a single pace forward. With a deafening crack and crunch, the ground under her feet began to give way. "Sam!" she cried. "Help!"

Sam reached out to grab his friend's hand, but only managed to brush her fingertips as she slid away, deeper into the caves.

The entire cave shook as rocks of all shapes and sizes broke away from the walls and ceiling and tumbled down after Alissa. Sam threw his hands into the air and clutched at the overhanging rock, hoping that he would not be swept off his own feet, too.

And then it was all over. The rocks stopped crashing, and the only sounds were the HISSSSS of falling dust, and Sam's own heart, thumping in his chest.

"Ali?" he called out, turning his torch in the direction the rocks had fallen. Silence.

Sam took a deep breath. What should he do? Go and look for Alissa in case she was hurt, or get help? His parents would be really angry about him going so far into the caves… but that didn't matter. What mattered was Alissa.

Sam turned to leave, but then he heard a voice. "Help!"

"Alissa!" he yelled. "Where are you?"

"Down here!" came the reply.

"Can you climb back up?"

"No," Alissa called out. "My leg's trapped."

"I'm going to get help!" said Sam.

"Wait!" shouted Alissa. "Don't do that! We'll get into trouble."

"You're already in trouble!" Sam pointed out.

"Not if you come down here and get me out," said Alissa. "Look – I'm sorry for messing about, but you should see it down here! It's amazing!"

Sam paused for a second. "Really?"

"Honestly!" said Alissa. "If we get grown-ups involved they'll seal up the entrance to the caves, and we'll never get the chance to see this ever again."

"Alright," said Sam with a sigh. "But, if you're winding me up again—"

"I'm not! Come down and help me!"

So, taking each step very carefully, Sam began to pick his way deeper into the caves. His torch showed that the rocks had all fallen down a steep tunnel. He pressed his hands against the sides of the passageway to stop himself from falling.

Eventually, he came to a pile of rocks blocking the end of the tunnel. He swung his torch upwards, and spotted a small gap near the ceiling.

"Ali? Are you through there?" he asked.

"Yes," Alissa replied. "You'll have to climb over – but be careful!"

"OK," said Sam. He took a deep breath, gripped his torch between his teeth and began to scale the pile of rocks.

There was another HISSSSS of dust, and one of the rocks wobbled beneath his foot but, before long, Sam was able to squeeze himself through the gap and climb down the other side.

Chapter 2

Blast!

Sam found himself in a vast underground cavern. Colourful stalagmites and stalactites dotted the floor and ceiling and a huge, black lake stretched into the darkness. "Wow!" he exclaimed.

Wow… Wow… Wow…

His voice echoed back from distant walls.

"Ali?"

Ali… Ali… Ali…

"Over here!"

Here… Here… Here…

Sam picked his way carefully across the cavern floor until he found his friend lying on the ground. A large rock had fallen onto one of her legs.

"You'll have to push this thing off me," said Alissa. "I can't do it from this angle."

"OK," said Sam. "I'll try…." Passing his torch to Alissa, he pressed his palms against the side of the rock and pushed as hard as he could. His friend grunted in pain as the boulder began to shift, and then it rolled off her leg completely.

"Phew!" said Alissa as Sam helped her back to her feet. "Thanks!"

"Is anything broken?" Sam asked.

Alissa shook her head. "I don't think so," she said. "Just sore. I'll be able to climb back out."

"Come on, then," Sam urged. "Before there's another rockfall!"

The children cautiously made their way back towards the tunnel, when Sam's torch caught something on the cave wall. It was the shape of an animal – some kind of deer by the look of it – painted in a dark red colour.

"Ali!" he hissed. "Come and look at this…."

Alissa's torchlight wobbled as she limped over to join him. "What is it?"

Alissa added her torch beam to her friend's, and they stepped back to reveal that the painting of the deer was just one of several. There were other pictures, too – human figures chasing the deer with spears, a mammoth, and even an animal with long, pointed teeth.

"These are cave paintings!" said Alissa, eyes wide with excitement. "We might be the first people to see these pictures in thousands of years!"

"I wonder who made them?" said Sam.

Alissa shrugged in the darkness. "Whoever lived here, I suppose."

"Look!" said Sam, moving his torch along the wall. "Maybe it was these people...."

The children stared at their new discovery – two red handprints pressed into the rocky wall, one slightly larger than the other.

"They're kids' handprints!" said Sam, pulling off his glove. "Look – the biggest one is the same size as my hand!"

"And the other is like mine," said Alissa. "Maybe whoever did these paintings were children – just like us!"

Reaching forward, Sam and Alissa pressed their palms against the ancient prints at exactly the same time.

The rock started to glow and get warmer. There was a loud whooooshing sound and the cave seemed to shimmer and shake. Everything went dark for a second, then there was a blinding flash of red, green and blue light. The two friends both screamed out loud as they found themselves falling… falling. Then, just as suddenly, they were back on their feet. They were standing outside the entrance of a cave – in the sunshine!

"Whoah!" said Alissa squinting. "I think I might have hit my head when I fell! There's suddenly a bright light in the sky."

"That's the sun!" breathed Sam.

"You can't have a sun inside a cave," Alissa reminded him.

"I know that," Sam said. "But we're not inside the cave any more…."

Alissa turned to look around. They were indeed standing in the mouth of a cave – and everything outside was lush, green grassland. Huge trees with strange leaves were dotted around. Insects buzzed in the air, and a gentle breeze blew – but did little to cool the stifling hot day.

"Where are we?" asked Alissa, pulling off her jacket.

"I don't think that's the right question," said Sam, shrugging off his own coat. "I think we should be asking '*When* are we?'"

Alissa blinked. "What?"

"I think we're in exactly the same place," said Sam. "But we've somehow travelled back in time."

"Don't be ridiculous!" scoffed Alissa.

"Well, can you think of a better explanation?"

"No… maybe you're right," Alissa agreed. "Well, come on!" she said, stepping out into the long grass.

"Wait!" said Sam, grabbing her arm. "Where are you going?"

"To explore," said Alissa. "I don't know how we got here, or how long this will last – but I'm going to make the most of it." Then she plunged on towards the nearest trees, her limp now forgotten.

Sam hurried after her, his eyes darting around as he tried to take everything in. "OK," he said eventually. "If we've really travelled back in time… how far back do you think?"

"What do you mean?"

"Well, are we going to see any dinosaurs?" Sam wondered aloud. "Or are they already extinct?"

"GRRRRRRRRRRRRRRR!!"

Alissa froze on the spot. "What was that?" she hissed.

"*That* was the answer to my question," Sam whispered back. "I reckon we've travelled back around 25,000 years."

Alissa scowled. "How can you tell?"

Sam pointed to a shape moving slowly through the grass towards them. It was a large animal covered in thick yellow fur. Huge, sharp fangs stuck out from the sides of its mouth. The creature fixed its piercing green eyes on the trembling children.

"Because that's when sabre-toothed cats lived in this part of the world!"

Chapter 3

Run!

Sam and Alissa slowly backed away as the giant cat padded towards them through the long, waving grass. The creature was in no hurry, knowing it could easily outrun the two children. It growled deep within its throat.

Sam reached out and found Alissa's hand. Her palm was as hot and sweaty as his own. "It's… so big!" he hissed. "Bigger than the lions and tigers at the safari park. What are we going to do?"

Alissa gave his hand a squeeze. "We have to get out of here," she said, "but, as calmly as possible. Any sudden moves, and that thing could pounce."

Sam felt tears pricking at the corners of his eyes. "I don't want to die," he croaked. "Not here. Not like this."

"Ssshhh," said Alissa. "It'll be OK."

"You don't know that!" said Sam, not taking his gaze off the approaching beast. "I mean – what happens if we die here in caveman times? Will we still be born in our own time period?"

"I don't know," Alissa admitted. "I've never time travelled before."

By now, the sabre-toothed cat was so close the children could feel its foul breath on their faces, and see their own terrified reflections in its mesmerizing, green eyes. The animal sank down on its haunches, rear end waving gracefully from side to side.

"I think it's playing with us," whispered Alissa as the creature bared its teeth and ran a long, pink tongue across its lips.

"Well, I'm not exactly in the mood for games right now!" hissed Sam.

"Not like that," said Alissa. "Like house cats when they catch a mouse or something. They play with it and tease it before the final attack. This is our last chance. We have to get away *now*!"

Suddenly, Alissa felt her back bump against something hard. Releasing Sam's hand, she reached behind and ran her fingers over the warm stone of the cave entrance. "It's the cave!" she said. "Maybe we can hide inside."

"If that thing doesn't jump on us first," said Sam.

"We need to distract it for a second," suggested Alissa. "Have you got anything you can throw at it?"

Sam slowly slid a hand into the pocket of his trousers. "Just my mobile phone," he said. "But if I lose that, my mum will kill me."

"She may have to join the queue!" said Alissa. Tearing her eyes away from the prowling predator, she spotted a rock on the ground and gently bent to pick it up. Her fingers scrabbled in the dust for a second, then she found the heavy stone and wrapped her hand around it.

Sensing that its prey was planning to fight back, the cat narrowed its fearsome eyes and snarled. Its muscles tensed like a tightly coiled spring.

"This is it!" breathed Alissa, slowly standing up again. "It's going to attack!" She felt the sharp points of the heavy stone in her grasp, and prepared to throw it as soon as the animal made its move.

Suddenly, a loud shout echoed out from somewhere over to the children's left. The sabre-toothed cat's attention was broken. Its head twisted to one side, eyes scanning the grass for any sign of danger.

Then, a long spear hurtled through the air, aiming for the angry animal.

The weapon's tip – made of sharp, polished stone – glinted in the bright sunlight, but missed its intended target.

Instead, the wooden handle of the spear clattered against the side of the cat's head. Fortunately, that was enough to scare the creature and, with a final snarl, it turned and ran away.

Sam sank down against the cave wall, finally allowing himself to breathe deeply. Alissa dropped the stone from her trembling hand and sighed.

Another shout in the distance made Sam and Alissa look up again. Perhaps the danger wasn't over yet. Striding towards them through the thick grass were two children who appeared to be around the same age as themselves. They wore ragged clothes made from animal hide, and their grimy skin was bronzed by the heat of the sun.

"Cave kids!" gasped Sam.

Alissa noticed that the taller of the two children – a boy – was carrying a spear just like the one that had been hurled at the sabre-toothed cat. The other child was a girl, and she had the same oval eyes as the boy. They were brother and sister.

"They're the ones who saved us!" said Alissa, taking a step forward.

Sam grabbed her arm. "What are you doing?" he demanded.

"Thanking them," Alissa replied.

"But, they could be dangerous, too."

Alissa looked the newcomers up and down. "They don't look dangerous…."

"Appearances can be deceptive, Ali," Sam pointed out. "I say we don't get involved, and just go home."

"I'd love to go home!" snapped Alissa. "But, I don't know how to – and neither do you! These kids could be able to help us find a way."

She turned back to the two young cave dwellers. "Hello, thanks for–" she began, but Sam pulled her back again.

"What now?!"

"You can't just talk to them," said Sam. "They're ancient savages. They won't understand."

"Then, how do you suggest we communicate with them?"

Sam smiled, for what felt like the first time in ages. "Watch and learn…."

Taking a step forward, he stretched both his arms out wide. "WE… FRIENDS!" he shouted, beginning to wave his hands mysteriously. "WE COME FROM… BIG SCARY FUTURE… WITH HUGE METAL

BIRDS IN SKY AND… MANY
GAMES ON PLAYSTATION
CONSOLE!"

The two cave children glanced at each other, frowning.

"OK, even basic language is too much for them," Sam whispered in Alissa's direction. "I'll try something simpler…."

Fixing a smile on his face, Sam began to act out what had happened to him and Alissa ever since finding the secret, hidden cave. He mimed climbing over the rockfall to get to his friend, looking at the cave paintings, being blasted through time and – finally – facing the sabre-toothed cat.

He was on all fours, stuffing twigs into the corners of his mouth to look like fangs when the cave boy spoke up.

"Is your friend unwell?" he asked Alissa. "I think he may have been outside in the sun too long."

He talked in a strange language but, somehow, Alissa and Sam could understand him.

Alissa grinned as Sam froze on the spot. "You *can* talk!" she said. "I knew it!"

"Of course we can," said the girl with a smile. She turned to Sam as he stood and tossed the twigs away. "And we're *not* savages…."

Sam looked down at his feet and kicked the ground, sheepishly.

Chapter 4

Friends

"My name's Moon," said the girl. "And this is my brother, Rock."

"Alissa and Sam," said Alissa.

"And this is our cave," explained Moon as she led them inside.

"Do you live here?" asked Sam.

Rock nodded. "Us two, and our mother and father."

"Where are your parents?" Alissa asked.

Rock took a quick look up at the sun in the sky. "Around this time, they'll be out hunting, and gathering food for our evening meal."

"We cook our meals there," said Moon, pointing to a ring of stones with a mound of burned ashes inside. "And we sleep at the back of the cave, where nothing can get to us."

"Hang on," said Sam, holding up his hands. "I still haven't worked out how we can be talking to each other yet. We shouldn't be able to understand a word!"

"We shouldn't be able to travel back in time from the future either," Alissa pointed out. "But, we did!"

"You're from the future?" said Rock, his eyes wide.

Alissa nodded. "Although we don't know why we're here, or how to get back there."

"The Shaman might be able to help," Moon suggested to her brother.

"Shaman?' said Alissa.

"He's a wise old man who people go to with their problems," Rock explained. "He lives about a day's walk from here."

"Can we go and see him?" asked Sam.

"Of course," Rock replied. "But it's too late to set off now. We'll go at first light in the morning."

"I guess that means we'll be spending the night in a cave!" said Alissa with a grin.

"I can show you how to make fire," said Rock. "But I'll have to wait until my father returns from the hunt."

"I'm going to be a hunter one day!" cried Moon, snatching the spear from Rock's hand and waving it around. "I was the one who threw the spear at that cat!"

"You missed!" said Rock, smiling.

"Not really," said Alissa. "You scared that thing away and saved us. Thank you!"

Suddenly, a loud wailing noise rang out.

"Mumba!" cried Moon. "It sounds as if she's in trouble!" Dropping the spear, Moon raced out of the cave. Rock, Sam and Alissa gave chase.

They followed the young cave girl as she dashed through the long grass which quickly grew taller than them. Soon, the group found themselves running through thicker bushes. Dense clumps of leaves rubbed at their sides and tickled their faces, and the warm dew on the branches sprayed them from head to toe. Sam thought it was a bit like going through a prehistoric car wash.

Eventually, they reached a small clearing – and both Sam and Alissa skidded to a halt. Moon was in the centre of the grass area.

"Where's your friend?" asked Alissa.

Instead of answering, Moon put her fingers to her mouth and let out a loud whistle. With a rustle, a furry trunk appeared from the trees in front of them, followed by a large furry face. A giant woolly mammoth stepped out of the forest towards them.

"Quick, run!" yelped Sam.

"No, it's ok," said Moon with a grin. "This is Mumba."

"Sh-she's a… mammoth?" mumbled Sam.

"Yes, a baby mammoth," beamed Moon.

Alissa stepped towards the animal as Moon began to cuddle it's trunk. Despite apparently being very young, it still towered above her head. She ran her fingers over the mammoth's woolly hide, and was surprised to discover how warm and soft it was. "Just like petting my cat at home."

"You can't do that to a cat!" cried Rock. "It would rip your hand off!"

Alissa giggled. "Cats are a lot smaller and friendlier where we come from."

"What about mammoths?" asked Moon. "Are they smaller, too?"

Alissa and Sam exchanged a worried glance. Could they really tell their new friends that mammoths were extinct in the modern day? Before they had a chance to reply, a stone whizzed through the air and hit Mumba on the side. She trumpeted a cry of pain.

"Oh no!" hissed Rock, crouching and looking around.

"What is it?" asked Alissa, joining him.

Rock pointed to a face peering at them from among the trees. It was covered in black and red paint, and made to look like some sort of demon.

Alissa squinted and spotted two more scary faces watching them.

Suddenly a spear launched from the bushes, landing dangerously close to Moon's bare foot.

"Who are they?" asked Sam.

"Older boys from another tribe," said Rock. "They call themselves the Shadows… and these kids really *are* savages."

"They're after Mumba!" cried Moon, her voice cracking.

"What for?" said Alissa.

Rock shrugged. "To prove they're great hunters," he said.

"You mean they want to… to kill Mumba?" Alissa gasped. "We can't let that happen."

Chapter 5

Scare

Alissa backed away, her eyes locked on the leader of the Shadows. His red-painted face was twisted with rage, and she saw that he was reaching for another spear. She somehow knew that his next shot wouldn't miss.

"We have to get Mumba out of here," she cried.

"No way. We're surrounded," said Rock. There were rustling sounds in the undergrowth all around them as more of the Shadows moved into position.

Soon the group of children would be surrounded. "We'll have to stand and fight!"

Rock snatched up a long branch which had fallen from one of the trees. Snapping it over his knee, he struck a battle pose, a length of wood clutched tightly in each hand.

"Fight?!" hissed Sam, trembling. "You may not have noticed – but there are four of us, and about twenty of them. And they've got catapults and rocks and spears and knives. Do you really think you can take them all on with just a couple of sticks?"

Slowly, spear held high, the Shadow boy with the demon face paint stepped out of the bushes and into the clearing. This was the cue for the rest of the hunters to do the same. Each held a lethal looking weapon of some sort. Alissa and Moon stood either side of Mumba, doing their best to shield her.

Rock scowled at Sam. "So, what's *your* plan, future boy?" he asked, stepping lightly from foot to foot, his eyes darting around as the Shadows approached on all sides.

"We use a little 21st-century magic!" said Sam. With that, he pulled his mobile phone from his pocket, hit the music app on the screen and held the gadget high above his head. Pop music instantly blasted out at full volume.

The Shadows froze at the sound, their eyes widening as the song's introduction began to build. They glanced nervously at each other as the lyrics started. When the bassline and drumbeat kicked in, they screamed in terror, turned and fled – melting back among the bushes as though they were never there at all.

The song still playing, Sam looked to the others – but he could only find Alissa. "Where are Moon and Rock?" he screamed over the music.

Alissa pointed to the long grass behind Mumba. Sam hurried over to discover the two cave children cowering in the foliage, with their hands clamped over their ears. He tapped the screen of his phone to pause the song.

"Are you OK?"

Slowly, Rock lowered his hands and looked up at him, terrified. "What was that?"

"That," said Sam, sliding the phone back into his pocket, "was music."

"No," said Rock, helping his sister to stand. "I know music. My family sings songs around the fire each evening. *That* sounded like the end of the world!"

Sam shrugged. "Well, it did the job. It scared the Shadows away."

"Well done, Sam," said Alissa. "I never would have thought of that."

"And that's why I'm the king of the Stone Age!" grinned Sam.

Suddenly, Mumba trumpeted loudly, making Sam jump. The other children giggled.

"Well, if you're quite finished, your majesty," teased Alissa, "maybe we should get this little one back to her family."

Rock and Moon led the way out of the jungle and onto a vast plain, covered with strange plants and exotic flowers. Mumba trotted along beside them as they walked.

"Look!" whispered Moon, grabbing Alissa's arm and pointing. Ahead of them a pack of woolly rhinos marched together towards a distant river where the slow-moving water glistened in the late afternoon sun.

Eventually, they found Mumba's herd. Alissa gasped. "Look at the size of those things!" she cried, staring at the adult mammoths. They were tearing huge clumps of foliage free from the ground with their trunks and stuffing them into their massive mouths.

"Can we get any closer?" asked Sam.

Rock shook his head. "Mumba may be used to being around people, but the rest of her herd are not. This is as close as we go."

Moon wrapped her arms as far as she could around the baby mammoth's neck, and planted a kiss on her forehead. "You're safe now!" she said. "Go and be with your family."

With a final trumpet, Mumba trotted off towards the other mammoths.

Chapter 6

Magic

Rock glanced up at the sky. The sun was falling steadily towards the distant hills. "We should go, too," he said. "It's dangerous to be out after nightfall, and our parents will be back soon. They'll wonder where we've got to."

By the time the group arrived at the cave, it was dusk. Millions of midges buzzed in the air, and the approaching night brought with it a chilling wind.

"Doesn't look as if your parents are home yet," said Alissa. The cave ahead of them was pitch black, the entrance gaping like a giant mouth caught forever in a prehistoric yawn.

"You know how to start fire don't you, Rock?" said Sam as he grabbed his coat from the ground where he had dropped it earlier.

"Yes, but my father will only allow me to do it when he is here," Rock replied. "He and my mother should not be much longer…."

Suddenly the entire interior of the cave was lit by a dozen flaming torches. The children were forced to shield their eyes from the fierce, yellow glow.

"Who's there?" called Rock, stepping protectively in front of his sister. Sam noticed the gesture, and quickly hid behind Alissa.

Slowly, five, ten – no, at least fifteen boys stepped out of the darkness, each one gripping a length of wood with a burning wad of material tied at the tip. Their faces were painted in red and black designs. They looked even scarier than they had before.

"The Shadows!" breathed Alissa.

Then a new figure appeared. He was an adult with ageing, leathery skin. Unlike the others around him, he wore no face paint, but that only made him all the more terrifying. The flickering flames from the boys' torches caused dark shadows to dance across his features.

"I think that's their tribe leader!" Rock hissed. "I've never seen him before… he rarely leaves their camp!"

"Well, something has got his attention," whispered Alissa. "And I think I know what, or rather, *who*, it is."

The man spoke. His voice was deep, and it echoed around the mouth of the cave. "Where is boy?" he demanded. "Boy make magic!"

There was a short pause, until....

"That's me," said Sam, stepping out from behind his friend.

The man nodded slightly. "Boy make magic... now!" he commanded.

Sam reached into his pocket for his phone, but Alissa grabbed his arm. "What are you doing?" she demanded.

"I'm going to scare them off again," Sam grinned.

Alissa glared at him. "Don't. It could be a trap!"

Sam pulled his arm free of her grasp. "You're just jealous," he said.

"Jealous? Of who?"

"Me of course!" Sam retorted. "You're jealous because you always think of yourself as the brave one… the brainy one… but it was *me* who saved us from the Shadows before, and I'm about to do it again!"

Before Alissa could reply, Sam held his phone up in the air and clicked play. Once more, thumping chart music pumped out of the speaker, causing everyone to cower back and cover their ears.

The man, however, did not flinch. He didn't seem afraid at all. Instead, he smiled, chanted a few words in his own language, and bowed deeply to Sam.

A few seconds later, the rest of his tribe dropped to their knees and did the same.

"Look at that," said Sam with a grin as he clicked off the music. "I *told* you I was the king of the Stone Age!"

"No…" said Rock slowly. "They think you're one of their tribe's guardian spirits come to life."

"Even better!" exclaimed Sam.

Standing, the man barked a series of orders to his teenage followers. Four of the boys quickly handed their torches to the person next to them and hurried over to hoist Sam onto their shoulders.

"This is fantastic!" said Sam. "Form a nice, orderly queue if you want an autograph!"

The man issued another string of garbled commands, then turned and began to stride away into the night. The teenagers carrying Sam hurried after him, followed by the torchbearers.

"Stop!" cried Alissa. "Sam, come back!"

"Don't worry!" Sam shouted. "If they want magic, I'll show them magic! I've got loads of great apps on my phone. They'll love them!"

"But we have to find the Shaman tomorrow," shouted Alissa. "We need to find a way home!"

"I've got to do this first, Alissa," Sam called. "I'm helping to make peace with the Shadow tribe!" He started the music up again. This time the hunters began to sway to the beat as they carried him aloft.

"Quickly!" urged Alissa, spinning to face Rock and Moon. Her eyes were wide with panic. "We have to go after them."

"We can't!" said Rock, firmly. "It's too dangerous to go away from the cave after dark."

"But this is different!" said Moon, looking anxiously at her brother. "They think he is a guardian spirit – and you know what that means…."

Rock stood firm. "It cannot be helped."

"What do you mean?" demanded Alissa, looking from Moon to Rock and back again. "So what if they think he's a spirit come to life?"

Moon took Alissa's hands in her own, and spoke quietly. "The Shadow tribe have a tradition," she explained. "In order to ensure good hunting and long life – they sacrifice anyone they believe to be a guardian spirit each day at noon."

Chapter 7

Lost

"They're going to *kill* Sam?" cried Alissa. "We have to follow the Shadows and rescue him right now!" she insisted. The flickering, orange lights of the hunters' flaming torches now looked like dancing fireflies in the distance.

"No," said Rock, firmly. "It's too dangerous. Our parents will be back soon. They will help us in the morning."

"But, Sam…" began Alissa.

"He went of his own accord," Rock reminded her. "They think he is one of their guardian spirits come to life. They'll treat him well."

"Until they sacrifice him at noon tomorrow, of course," Moon reminded them.

Alissa blinked back desperate tears. "Would you go after them if they'd taken Moon," she asked.

"Of course!" replied Rock. "She's my sister."

"And Sam's like a brother to me," said Alissa firmly. "He might act without thinking sometimes, and he can be a bit annoying – but he's my best friend, and I'm going to rescue him, whether you two come with me or not!"

With that, Alissa turned and marched off into the darkness after the Shadows.

Rock sat down and crossed his arms.

Moon stood beside him, watching their new friend disappear into the undergrowth. "Alissa won't be able to find their camp," she said.

"I know," said Rock. "But it's nothing to do with me."

"She will soon be lost… and in danger…."

"I warned her not to go. I said to wait until morning."

"But I like her… and she has no idea what she's doing…. There could be any number of wild beasts out there, searching for prey…."

"Oh, alright!" snapped Rock, jumping to his feet. "But *you* can explain this to mother and father when – *if* – we see them again!"

"Fine!" smiled Moon. "I'll fetch a torch while you start a fire." The young girl ran into the cave and returned with a torch very much like the ones the Shadows had been carrying.

Rock pulled a piece of flint and a stone from a pouch at his side. Tearing up a handful of dried grass and a few twigs, he piled up the kindling, then began to strike the stone with the edge of his flint. Sparks flew once, twice – then the kindling caught alight and started to give off smoke.

Rock dropped to his stomach beside the tiny flame and began to blow on it gently. The orange glow grew and, soon, the grass and twigs were crackling as they burned.

Moon dipped the head of the torch in

the flames and watched with satisfaction as it too began to burn. "Let's go!" she cried, dashing into the undergrowth.

After kicking earth over his tiny fire to put it out, Rock slipped his flint back into his pouch, then ran after his sister.

* * *

Alissa pushed her way through thick bushes in the moonlight, trembling as the cold air began to bite. What had been lush, green vegetation during the day looked all black and twisted in the darkness. Branches reached out to grab at her hair like long witch's fingers, and gnarled roots tripped her up again and again.

Suddenly, there was a whispering of wings and Alissa ducked as a flock of large birds – or were they giant bats – swept overhead, their moonlit shadows racing across the bleak vegetation like silent aeroplanes.

She stopped, and tried to get her bearings. The tiny pinpricks of light from the Shadows' torches had now completely disappeared. Alissa began to feel nervous. Was she just walking round and round in circles?

"The stars!" she said, looking up. "People used to navigate using the stars…." The night sky was a blanket of sparkling diamonds above her, with streaks of bold blue and lingering lilac marking out sections of the Milky Way galaxy. Without electric lights to pollute the planet, the stars looked amazing – but they didn't help Alissa work out which direction she should be travelling in. She was lost.

CRACK!

Alissa jumped as a twig snapped somewhere behind her. She wasn't alone! A hand grabbed Alissa's shoulder and spun her round.

It was Rock!

She flung her arms around the cave boy and hugged him tightly.

"Whoah!" Rock chuckled. "It's OK, you're safe now. Moon – I've found her!" he called.

A flickering glow came rushing towards them through the undergrowth, then Moon appeared with her torch. "Thank goodness!" she cried.

"I'm sorry," said Alissa. "I should have listened to you back at the cave."

"No," said Rock. "I should have listened to you. Sam is your friend – and our friend too. We have to help him."

"Do you know the way to the Shadows' camp from here?" Alissa asked.

Rock nodded. "It's not far," he replied. "Follow me – and stay together."

Chapter 8

Dance

Alissa, Rock and Moon reached the camp a little under an hour later. They put out their torch and hid behind a hut on the outskirts of the camp. The trio watched the festivities taking place in the central clearing. A roaring fire stretched up towards the sky as if it would burn the stars. A group of older men sat to one side, beating drums and singing in the Shadows' language.

Everyone else wore masks made to look like bizarre animals, and danced around the fire. Leaping and hopping from foot to foot, the dancers' hands slapped against their chests in time with the beat.

Older women and young children sat around the edges of the clearing, clapping along, chanting or just chatting together. The Shadows' teenage hunters duelled with spears and knives, laughing as they tumbled each other to the ground.

"I can't see Sam anywhere!" Alissa muttered.

"There!" whispered Moon, pointing through the twisting flames of the fire.

Alissa shifted to one side to get a better view – and gasped. On the other side of the fire was a large, rough-hewn wooden throne. Sam was sitting on it! He had a garland of flowers in his hair, and villagers were laying gifts of fruit, furs and jewellery made from bones at his feet. He was having a wonderful time!

"This is how they treat the human spirits the night before their sacrifice," said Rock grimly. "We have to get to him."

"But how?" asked Moon.

Alissa ran her fingers over the reed wall that made up the back of the nearest hut. She lifted it up, creating a small gap that they could crawl under. "I've got an idea!" she said, disappearing into the shelter. With a shrug, Rock and Moon followed.

* * *

The three 'new villagers' burst out of the hut, already dancing. They wore strange masks over their faces, and had daubed their skin with coloured paints.

Alissa had rolled up her trouser legs and shirtsleeves, and had draped a length of animal hide around her shoulders to hide her clothes.

The heat from the fire had them sweating within minutes as they copied the dance moves of those around them – all the while, circling round the clearing and getting closer to the throne. Alissa reached out, snatched up a rough wooden cup filled with water and spun around to the noise of the drums.

Before long, she was close enough to the throne to place the cup down at Sam's side. "For you…" she said from behind her mask.

"Thanks," said Sam, picking up the drink. "I don't suppose it's Dr Pepper, though!"

"You're in terrible danger!" hissed Alissa.

"I don't think so!" said Sam, grabbing a piece of fruit and biting down hard. "I'm a lucky spirit, don't you know!"

He jumped as two more masks appeared beside him. "We must flee, now!" said the taller of the two dancers.

"Follow us!" urged the other.

Sam frowned. "I thought you lot were supposed to worship me, not tell me to leave?"

With a frustrated grunt, Alissa grabbed the bottom of her mask and lifted it far enough for Sam to see her face. "It's us, you moron! We've come to rescue you!" She quickly lowered the mask again and continued to dance beside the throne.

"Alissa?" cried Sam. "What are you – hang on, rescue me from what?"

"STOP!" roared an angry voice.

Instantly, the drums ceased and the entire tribe stopped dancing. Now the only noises were the spitting of the fire, and the footsteps of the village leader as he strode towards the throne.

He ripped Alissa's mask from her face, then did the same to Rock and Moon. "Outsiders!" he growled.

The teenage boys grabbed their spears and hurried forward.

"Oh, no…" sighed Rock.

"It's OK," said Sam, rising to his feet. "I'll handle this…."

Alissa groaned. "Sam, no…." But it was too late.

"My people…" announced Sam. "Big Shadows and little Shadows…. As one of your spirits come to life, I order you not to harm my three friends, but instead to treat them like ki–"

He didn't get any further. The tribal leader produced a handful of purple dust and blew it straight into Sam's face. Sam's eyes crossed, then he collapsed to the ground, out cold.

Alissa spun on the leader. "What have you done to him?" she cried, just as the man blew a cloud of dust at her.

The world shifted and blurred, and Alissa felt herself falling into a whirlpool of colour. Then everything turned black.

* * *

When Alissa woke, it was early dawn. She blinked hard against the emerging sunlight, and made to raise her hands to cover her eyes. But she couldn't, because they were tied behind her back to a wooden post that had been driven into the ground at the edge of a long drop into a valley below.

"She's awake," said a voice. Rock was tied to an identical post on her right. Moon was on her left. The Shadows were nowhere to be seen.

"This is terrible!" Alissa groaned.

"It's not so bad," said Rock with a smile.

"What?!" cried Alissa. "How can you stay so calm about all this?"

"Because – just before you woke up – I remembered the piece of flint on my pouch!"

"He's cutting himself loose now," said Moon.

"There!" said Rock, freeing his hands. He hurried over to untie Alissa.

"What about the Shadows?" she asked.

"I don't suppose they thought we'd need guarding once they'd tied us up," said Moon. "But, we'd better hurry and get away from here quickly."

Alissa's hands were suddenly free, and she rubbed at the red marks left on her wrists. "Yes we have to get back to Sam!"

"No," said Rock.

"But you said you were going to help me!" Alissa cried. "You said he was your friend too!"

"He is," agreed Rock, "and I'll keep my word. But going back to the Shadows' camp isn't the way to do that."

"Wh-what do you mean?" asked Alissa.

"We need to find the Shaman. I'm sure he will be able to fix everything. But we'd better get a move on," Rock urged, looking up at the sun. "We don't have much time." He headed towards the cliff edge.

"What are you doing?" gasped Moon.

"This is the quickest way to the Shaman," explained Rock. "We need to climb down into the valley, then follow the river to the Sacred Mountain."

"Are you serious?" said Moon peering over the edge at the sheer drop beneath.

"We'll be fine," said Rock, stretching his legs over the edge and onto a thin ledge below. "There are plenty of hand- and footholds."

Raising her eyebrows at Moon, Alissa followed Rock down into the valley, gripping tightly to the cliff face as she slowly made her way down. After a minute she looked up, but Moon wasn't following her.

"What are you doing?" Alissa called. "We need to hurry."

"I can't do it," cried Moon. "I'm scared of heights."

"Get down here right now!" boomed Rock.

"Don't worry I'll be fine," said Moon, a grin lighting up her face. "I have an idea – a backup plan. You find the Shaman, and I'll meet you back at the Shadows' camp to rescue Sam."

"No, wait!" called Rock, but Moon had already disappeared.

"Brilliant," said Alissa, climbing level with Rock. "So it's just you and me."

"Not exactly," murmured Rock.

Chapter 9

Slide!

Rock and Alissa clung to the side of the cliff face, toes resting on a thin ledge and fingers clutching tightly to jagged lumps of stone that jutted out from the precipice. Strong gusts of wind threatened to drag them away from the cliff and hurl them down to the grassland below.

"We've got company…" replied Rock.

"What?!" Alissa slowly turned her face to look down at the ground. There, ducking and weaving through the long grass below were a dozen figures. From this height, they looked a bit like mice finding their way through a maze – but Alissa knew exactly what they were.

"The Shadows!" she hissed.

"They'll reach the bottom of the cliff before we can," said Rock. "We'll have to climb back up…."

"GRRRRRRRRR!"

The kids peered up at the top of the rock wall to see a sabre-toothed cat snarling back down at them. The animal paced up and down, eyeing its prey hungrily.

"I don't think that's going to work, either," said Alissa flatly.

"What shall we do?" asked Rock.

"I guess we have to choose," said Alissa. "Up or down. Sabre-toothed cat in one direction, gang of angry hunters in the other."

"It's not much of a choice," said Rock.

"No, but it's the only one we've got," Alissa pointed out. "And we'll have to choose quickly; my hands are starting to go numb."

"GRRRRRRRRRR!"

Above them, the large cat swiped a massive paw over the cliff edge. Long, razor-sharp claws glinted in the sun like knives.

"I vote for down," said Rock, swallowing hard. "There may be more of the Shadows, but at least we can try to reason with them."

Rock and Alissa continued their climb down the cliff face. They moved slowly, testing each footrest and handhold before committing their entire weight. Below, the young hunters were now gathered together in a group, their horrifically painted faces turned upwards as they chanted and shouted in their own language.

Suddenly, an arrow pinged off the stone beside Rock's face. "The Shadows are firing up at us!" he cried. "I'm not sure we'll be able to reason with them, after all."

"We may not have to," said Alissa. "Look…."

She nodded her head to the right. Rock followed her gaze. There, carved into the cliff was a small cave entrance.

Another arrow clipped the wall near Alissa's hand. "We can hide in there and think of a plan!"

The pair began to move towards the opening as quickly as they could. Below, the Shadows spotted what they were trying to do and began to fire more rapidly. Before long, spears were clattering off the rocks around them as well as arrows.

Alissa was just climbing into the mouth of the cave when….

"Aargh!"

"Rock!" she cried. Alissa reached out to grab her friend's hand, and pulled him into the cave. They fell to the stone floor, gasping for breath.

"One of the arrows caught my arm," he said, wincing,

Alissa peered at the wound in the dim light of the cave. "It's bleeding pretty badly," she said. "And here we are, thousands of years before the invention of the bandage."

"You could use a spider's web!" came a shrill voice behind them.

Alissa and Rock spun round to find a strange man emerging out of the darkness, hopping from one bare foot to the other. He had a piece of dirty animal skin around his waist, and a long beard that reached almost down to his knees. Balanced on top of his head was a bird's nest, from which three tiny chicks were cheeping.

Alissa and Rock watched as he swept his hand through the air near the roof of the cave, lifting away an entire spider's web. He stopped hopping and slapped the web over Rock's wound. Instantly, the bleeding began to slow.

"That should do it!" cackled the man as he began hopping again.

"Who *are* you?" asked Rock.

"That is a very good question!" replied the man. "There are those who know me as the Shaman… but most people just call me Shay."

"We've been looking for you!" Alissa exclaimed.

"And now you've found me," beamed Shay. Suddenly, he froze and a look of terror washed over his features. "Have you come to steal my birds?"

"No!" said Alissa. "Of course not! We came because we need your help getting home – to the future."

"THE FUTURE!" wailed Shay mysteriously, his eyes flitting from left to right. Then he grinned and resumed his hopping. "Yep, I can do that. But, we'll have to rescue your friend first...."

Alissa gasped. "How do you know about Sam?"

The Shaman shrugged. "The same way I know that the Shadows are currently climbing up the cliff to get to you."

Rock risked a glance out of the cave and saw that the strange man was right. The teenage hunters were steadily climbing towards the opening.

"We need to get out of here, now!" said Shay.

"Using magic?" asked Rock.

Shay shook his head. "No – using a trapdoor." The old man pushed a stone into a hole in the wall and a small opening appeared in the floor. "Quick!"

he urged, ushering Alissa towards it. "Get down there!"

Alissa dropped through the gap as the first of the face-painted Shadows reached the mouth of the cave. She expected to land in some sort of underground cavern but, instead, found herself sliding down a chute of smooth, polished stone.

Faster and faster she slid in the darkness, twisting first left, then right. She tucked her hands into her sides and lay back to pick up extra speed.

"Wow!"

Alissa heard Rock's voice as he too began his descent, followed by the incessant cheeping of baby birds. The Shaman was right behind them.

A light began to glow up ahead,

allowing Alissa to see that she was racing towards the end of the bizarre slide. A few seconds later, she came whooshing out of a gap near the ground and landed on a soft pile of dried grass.

Rock tumbled out of the tunnel beside her. "We're right outside the Shadows' camp!" he said, looking around.

"Wheeeeeeeeeeee!" Shay shot out of the slide, hovered in the air for a moment and then landed neatly on his feet. "It won't take those spear-happy fools long to find where we've gone," he said. "We have to get to Sam as soon as possible!"

Rock looked up at the position of the sun in the sky. "It's almost noon!" he said.

"Let's go!" cried Alissa.

"Wait!" yelled the Shaman.

They watched as Shay pulled a handful of wriggling worms from somewhere in his beard and fed them to the chicks on his head.

"OK," he said. "Now, I'm ready!"

Chapter 10

Print

The trio dodged between huts and sprinted into the clearing in the centre of the Shadows' camp.

"There he is!" said Alissa, pointing.

Sam was tied to his wooden throne – which was now balanced on top of a huge pile of sticks. The warriors of the tribe were dancing around it, chanting and clutching flaming torches.

"OK, guys!" Sam shouted. "Enough is enough. I think I'd like to go home now...."

"Sam!" cried Alissa as she and Rock dashed towards her friend.

Shay pulled a long, green vegetable out of his beard and began to wield it like a sword. "Stay back!" he warned the confused tribe. "I know how to use this thing!"

"Ali'!" Sam yelled. "Get me out of here!"

"That's what we're trying to do!" Alissa replied – then someone grabbed her arm and spun her round. It was the Shadows' aged tribe leader. He glared down at her.

"No take boy!" he snarled.

"But he's my friend!" argued Alissa. "I won't let you hurt him!"

The leader barked an order in his own language and several young men sprang forward to hold Alissa and Rock firmly in place. Another pair took hold of Shay, knocking his vegetable to the ground.

They could do nothing but watch as the warriors lowered their torches and set the bonfire alight.

"NO!' bellowed Sam, struggling against the ropes that tied him to the throne. "PLEASE, NO!"

The flames licked higher and higher. Alissa could feel their heat pricking her skin. She turned her head away, unable to watch Sam fighting to be free. There was nothing she could do.

"CHARGE!"

The ground began to shake as a huge herd of mammoths burst into the camp trumpeting loudly. Leading the assault was Mumba – with Moon sitting on her back! The mammoths smashed through the huts, trampling them to the ground with their colossal feet.

The Shadow tribe ran, screaming, as their camp was pounded into the ground. Two of the largest mammoths began to attack the bonfire with their long, pointed tusks. The pile of burning wood leaned first one way, then the other.

Rock clambered up onto the back of one of the giant beasts, grabbing handfuls of hair to help him climb. Finding his balance, he pulled out his flint and quickly cut Sam free.

"Jump!" he ordered as the throne started to fall.

Sam and Rock hit the ground hard as the roaring bonfire disintegrated. Instantly, the mammoths began to squirt water from their trunks onto the flames, extinguishing the fire.

"Sam!" cried Alissa, throwing her arms around her friend. "I thought I'd lost you!"

"No chance!" said Sam with a wink.

The Shaman appeared at their side. "There's no time to lose!" he cried, chewing hard on something. "Give me your hands…."

Both Sam and Alissa held out their palms – and the Shaman spat a lump of sticky, red gloop onto them.

"Yuk!" said Sam. "That's horrible!"

"It's your way home… and yes… it's horrible," said Shay, his eyes flitting around again. "You must go now!"

"Jump on!" cried Moon, racing over to them on Mumba.

Rock helped Alissa and Sam climb up onto the back of the woolly creature, then jumped up himself.

"Can she carry all four of us?" Alissa asked.

"Just you watch!" beamed Moon. She tapped at the baby mammoth's sides with her heels, and they set off at a run, the rest of Mumba's herd trumpeting their goodbyes.

"Farewell, my fabulous future friends!" shouted Shay, now hopping from one foot to the other again. "Make prints, and you'll be home before you know it!"

"Who is that weird bloke?" Sam asked, staring at the red gloop in the middle of his palm. "And what's this stuff he spat all over us?"

"It's paint," said Alissa with a smile, holding her own hand carefully so as not to lose its contents. "And I think I know what to do with it."

Mumba raced all the way back to Rock and Moon's cave, where they found their parents waiting anxiously for them.

"Where have you been all night?" demanded their mother as Moon jumped down to hug her.

"We had a problem with the Shadows," Rock explained.

"The Shadows?" said their father. "That tribe is trouble."

"It's OK," said Rock. "Thanks to our new friends, they won't bother us any more."

"Hello children," smiled the cave mum. "By your strange clothing, I think you must be from a far away tribe."

"Very far away," said Alissa.

"And near at the same time," added Sam.

"Do you really have to go?" asked Moon.

Alissa nodded. "The Shaman said we must act straight away."

"He was babbling on about a prince or something," Sam reminded her.

"No, *'prints'*," said Alissa, rolling her eyes. "He meant *hand* prints, Sam!"

Sam's eyes grew wide. "Like the ones we touched to get here!" He ran inside the cave and studied the wall. "They're not there!"

Alissa hurried over to him. "That's because we have to leave them behind!"

"Huh?" said Sam. "So, we magically came here by touching the hand prints we'd left behind twenty-five thousand years earlier?"

Alissa shrugged. "I guess so!"

Suddenly, the red paint in their hands began to sparkle. Flashes of scarlet and crimson raced across their palms.

"This is it!" said Alissa. "Ready?"

Sam nodded. "Ready!"

"Goodbye!" said Rock.

"We'll always remember you!" said Moon.

Sam and Alissa pressed their paint-filled palms to the cave wall.

There was a flash of red, green and blue light just like before. But this time the children felt themselves flying, not falling. Suddenly they were standing, alone, in a darkened cave.

Alissa looked around. "Did it work?" she asked. "Are we back?"

BEEP BEEP! BEEP BEEP!

Sam pulled out his phone. "It's a text from my dad," he said, tapping the screen. "He wants to know if you'd like to come round for a barbecue tonight."

Alissa beamed. "We're definitely back!" she sighed. "And I'm starving. A barbecue sounds great!"

"It really does!" agreed Sam, sliding his phone back into his pocket. His fingers brushed against something else in there. Something cold, hard and sharp. He lifted Rock's piece of flint up into the shaft of light.

"And I know just how to light it!"

THE END

FICTION EXPRESS

THE READERS TAKE CONTROL!

Have you ever wanted to change the course of a plot, change a character's destiny, tell an author what to write next?

Well, now you can!

'Blast to the Past' was originally written for the award-winning interactive e-book website Fiction Express.

Fiction Express e-books are published in gripping weekly episodes. At the end of each episode, readers are given voting options to decide where the plot goes next. They vote online and the winning vote is then conveyed to the author who writes the next episode, in real time, according to the readers' most popular choice.

www.fictionexpress.co.uk

WINNER
Education Resources
Award for Innovation

FICTION EXPRESS

TALK TO THE AUTHORS

The Fiction Express website features a blog where readers can interact with the authors while they are writing. An exciting and unique opportunity!

FANTASTIC TEACHER RESOURCES

Each weekly Fiction Express episode comes with a PDF of teacher resources packed with ideas to extend the text.

"The teaching resources are fab and easily fill a whole week of literacy lessons!"
Rachel Humphries, teacher at Westacre Middle School

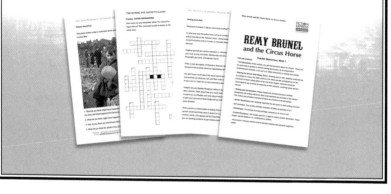

The Sand Witch
by Tommy Donbavand

When twins Chris and Ella are left to look after their younger brother on a deserted beach, they expect everything to be normal, boring in fact. But then something extraordinary happens! Will the Sand Witch succeed in passing on her sandy curse in this exciting adventure?

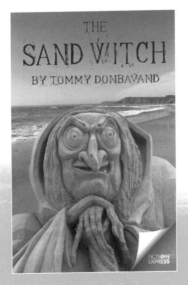

ISBN 978-1-78322-544-6

FICTION EXPRESS

Rise of the Rabbits
by Barry Hutchison

When twins Harvey and Lola are given the school rabbit, Mr Lugs, to look after for the weekend, they're both very excited. That is until the rabbit begins to mutate and decides the time has come for bunnies to rise up and seize control.

It's up to Harvey and Lola to find a way to return Mr Lugs and his friends to normal, before the menaces sweep across the country – and then the world!

ISBN 978-1-78322-540-8

FICTION EXPRESS

Curious Cal and the Wish Machine
by Cavan Scott

When Cal is forced to spend time with his elderly next-door-neighbour, Mr Patel, he thinks he's in for a boring time. But nothing could be further from the truth. What will happen when Cal is let loose in Mr Patel's laboratory of mad and marvellous machines? And can the wish machine really give Cal what he desires?

ISBN 978-1-78322-595-8

FICTI●N EXPRESS

The Vampire Quest
by Simon Cheshire

James is an ordinary boy, but his best friend Vince is a bit... odd. For one thing, it turns out that Vince is a vampire. His parents are vampires, too. And so are the people who live at No. 38. There are vampires all over the place, it seems, but there's nothing to worry about. They like humans, and they'd never, ever do anything... horrible to them. Unless... the world runs out of Feed-N-Gulp, the magical vegetarian vampire brew. Which is exactly what's just happened....

ISBN 978-1-78322-553-8

FICTION EXPRESS

Snaffles the Cat Burglar
by Cavan Scott

When notorious feline felon Snaffles and his dim canine sidekick Bonehead are caught red-pawed trying to steal the Sensational Salmon of Sumatra, not everything is what it seems. Their capture leads them on a top-secret mission for the Ministry of Secret Shenanigans.

Will Snaffles and Bonehead save the world or will everything come to a sticky end?

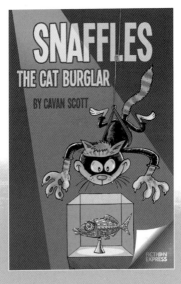

ISBN 978-1-78322-543-9

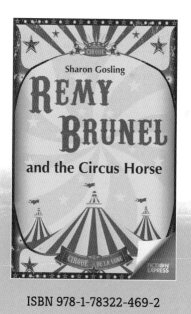

About the Author

Tommy is the author of the popular 13-book 'Scream Street' series for 7 to 10 year-olds. His other books include *Zombie!*, *Wolf* and *Uniform* (winner of the Hackney Short Novel Award). His books for Fiction Express include *The Sand Witch*, a story about a beach coming to life, and *Trouble in Withy Wood*, featuring a showdown between opposing armies of ancient creatures.

In theatre, Tommy's plays have been performed to thousands of children on national tours. These productions include 'Hey Diddle Diddle', 'Rumplestiltskin', 'Jack & Jill In The Forgotten Nursery', and 'Humpty Dumpty And The Incredibly Daring Rescue Of The Alien Princess From Deep Space'. He is also responsible for five episodes of the CBBC TV series, *Planet Cook* (Platinum Films).

Tommy lives in Lancashire with his wife and two sons. He is a HUGE fan of all things Doctor Who, plays blues harmonica, and makes a mean balloon poodle. He sees sleep as a waste of good writing time.